ISBN 978-1-78270-037-1

Text copyright © Award Publications Limited
Illustrations copyright © Val Biro

This edition published 2015

Published by Award Publications Limited, The Old Riding School,
The Welbeck Estate,Worksop, Nottinghamshire, S80 3LR

15 1

Printed in Malaysia

Magical Tales for Bedtime

by Linda Jennings

adapted by
Jackie Andrews and Sophie Giles

Illustrated by Val Biro

Award Publications Limited

Contents

The Witch's New Broomstick   8

The Last Wizard   12

The Lost Rabbit   15

Felicity Witch   18

The Daisy Ring   22

Playing Wizards   25

The Witch Trap   29

The Travelling Witch   33

The Spelling Book   37

Fairy Cakes   40

The Hallowe'en Party   43

The New Broom   47

Nat's Magic Seedling	50
The Broomstick Race	53
The Magic Bicycle	56
The Monster Under the Pavement	59
The Magic Stone	63
Cat on a Broomstick	66
Dragon Fire	69
The Little Yellow Goblin	73
The Troll in the Pool	76
All That Glitters	80
Not Quite a Dragon	83
Witch Twinkletoes	87
The Witch at the Bottom of the Lane	90

The Witch's New Broomstick

Witch Nightshade was flying high above Frightful Forest one night when her broomstick suddenly began to fall apart.

"Bother! Perhaps I shouldn't have used it to do my spring cleaning this morning," she mused as she swooped to the ground to examine it.

The old broomstick was clearly beyond repair. "Well, I can't get about without one," she grumbled to herself.

So the very next day Witch Nightshade marched into the shop in town to find herself a new broomstick.

"A broomstick?" said the shop assistant, shaking his head. "There's not much demand for those nowadays."

"But *I'm* demanding one," said Witch Nightshade.

"That's as may be," replied the shop assistant, "but I don't have any."

"Well, what am I to do?" wailed the witch. "I must have a broom! What do people use instead, then?"

"Vacuum cleaners."

"Really?" said Witch Nightshade, who had never heard of such a thing. "Perhaps I'd better see some of those, then, so bring them out, please." The man looked doubtfully at the witch, but did as he was asked.

"Oooh," said Witch Nightshade. "Aren't they lovely!" She headed straight for a streamlined green and beige model, thinking what a sensation she would cause with it in the coven. "I'll take it!" she told the assistant.

He told her the price, convinced it would be too much for this strange-looking lady dressed in rags.

Witch Nightshade took out a purse that appeared to be completely empty and, to the shop assistant's astonishment, pulled a huge handful of notes from it.

The shop assistant took the money and picked up a large cardboard box from behind the counter.

"Oh, there's no need to pack it," said Witch Nightshade. "I'll ride it home."

"Ride it?" exclaimed the puzzled shop assistant.

"Well, it's not quite what I'm used to," said the witch, "but surely it shouldn't be too difficult to handle." And, settling herself astride the handle of the cleaner, she zoomed out of the shop.

The poor shop assistant decided it must be time for a soothing cup of tea. He couldn't quite believe what he had just seen.

Witch Nightshade's new-fangled broomstick certainly caused a sensation: as soon as they saw it, all her witch friends wanted one for themselves!

And so the shop assistant was even more amazed when a whole gaggle of oddly-dressed ladies came later that day and bought every last one of his vacuum cleaners!

The Last Wizard

Believe it or not, the last magical wizard in the land was not a white-haired old gentleman but a little boy named Billy. Like all wizards, he was the seventh son of a seventh son.

For a time, Billy enjoyed it. Being a wizard made him very popular at school, because he could cast spells to make everyone's homework correct, and he could make sure that his football team always won their matches.

But gradually Billy grew tired of working spells for his friends. In fact, he wished he wasn't a wizard at all. He didn't like being different from the other children.

"I've decided I don't want to be a wizard any more,"
Billy told his parents one day as they were having
dinner. "I'm fed up with always being asked to cast
spells for people," he grumbled.

"Once a wizard, always a wizard," his mum reminded
him. "You ought to be pleased to be the only real
wizard left in the land."

Billy scowled and pushed his sausages round his plate.
He couldn't even be bothered to cast a spell to make
them jump up and dance.

In fact, Billy was so fed up that he confided in his best friend, Joe.

"I just don't know what to do," he said. "I've got this great big book of magic that makes me cast spells, even if I don't want to."

Joe had a brilliant idea. "How about I help you to get rid of it," he said. "I could borrow it and then sort of *lose* it?"

Billy knew his parents would be furious, but he was so desperate that he agreed.

So the next day Billy lent Joe the book and it immediately 'disappeared'. Without it, Billy felt quite relieved as he now couldn't work any spells at all. His parents were mad, of course, but nothing could be done.

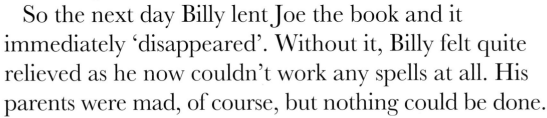

And what happened to the spell book? Thousands of miles away in Australia, Joe's aunt was celebrating her birthday. Eagerly she unwrapped the heavy parcel that arrived from her nephew.

"A book of spells!" she exclaimed in delight. "Just what I've always wanted!"

For what Joe didn't know was that his aunt was the seventh daughter of a seventh daughter!

The Lost Rabbit

On the day of Simon's birthday party his pet rabbit, Thumper, disappeared. Simon found the hutch door open and realised he couldn't have closed it properly.

Somehow, though, he felt sure Thumper had been stolen. How could he enjoy his party now? He was far too worried about Thumper.

When his friends arrived, all Simon could manage was the most watery of smiles. To make matters worse, his friend Carla gave him a special brush for grooming Thumper. Simon thanked her in a very small, wobbly voice.

He cheered up a little when everyone sang "Happy Birthday" and he blew out the candles on his cake.

And he brightened up even more when his mum annouced that there was to be a special surprise.

The children all fell silent as a mystical-looking character with a long golden wand swept into the room wearing a tall black hat and long blue robes decorated with silver stars.

A magician!

When the magician waved his wand the children all gasped, spellbound. And so began a wonderful display of magic. For his first trick, he transformed the flowery living room wallpaper into a real-live garden with the flowers blowing gently in the breeze.

Then a troupe of ballet dancers came twirling right out of the television!

And no sooner had the dancers vanished, than a dazzling firework display began right there in the middle of the room!

Finally, the magician produced a shiny, black top hat.

Turning to Simon he asked, "What would you like me to bring out of my magic hat for your birthday? Think about it very hard, but don't tell anyone what it is."

Simon shut his eyes and wished and wished.

The magician waved his wand, and out of his hat came…

"Thumper!" shouted Simon, recognising his beloved rabbit at once. Jumping up, he took Thumper from the magician and cuddled the rabbit in his arms.

Could the magician have stolen him? Simon didn't think so. He had used *real* magic, not just conjuring tricks. No, somehow the magician's magic had brought Thumper right back home from wherever he had been.

Simon never did find out how Thumper came to appear from the magician's hat, but he knew he couldn't have wished for a better birthday present, and when he went to bed that night his head was full of the most magical dreams!

Felicity Witch

Felicity Witch lived in an old cottage at the edge of the wood with her faithful cat, Midnight. She was a well-meaning and kindly witch who got on well with the local villagers. In fact, they were rather proud to have a witch living among them. But one day, she received a letter from Chief Witch Hemlock.

You are summoned to appear before the coven next Friday, 13th May, at midnight sharp. DON'T BE LATE!

Felicity trembled with worry. Being summoned by the Chief Witch usually meant trouble. But as far as Felicity knew, she hadn't done anything wrong.

She did have rather more visitors than was usual for a witch, it was true: every Tuesday afternoon she held a tea party for the ladies in the village. They loved Felicity's blackberry tea, and were all very fond of her, despite her odd appearance.

Felicity arrived early at the coven and greeted her sister witches with her usual sweet smile. They smiled back cheerfully, which made Felicity Witch feel better. Perhaps she wasn't in trouble after all.

Then Chief Witch Hemlock arrived. She was a tall, skinny, bad-tempered witch with piercing black eyes and a hairy chin.

Seeing all the witches smiling and talking together, she flew furiously into the middle of the gathering.

"This is all your doing, Felicity Witch!" she screeched.

"What is?" asked Felicity.

"All this laughing and being nice. It's just not witch-like," said the Chief Witch sourly. "It has to stop!"

"But I can't stop," said Felicity. "Even my name means 'happiness'!"

"Then we'll just have to change your name," said Chief Witch Hemlock. "We'll call you… Wartsnap!"

Felicity stopped smiling. "That's an ugly name!"

"Too bad!" said Chief Witch Hemlock. "At least you're not smiling any more! I'm Chief Witch, so what I say, goes!"

Poor Felicity flew home in tears.

Her horrible new name made her so miserable that now she could hardly smile at all.

On Tuesday afternoon, when the ladies from the village came round as usual, they found Felicity hunched, haggard and unhappy.

"Cheer up," they said, giving her a hug. "Give us one of your lovely smiles." Felicity managed just a tiny one. "You can do better than that!" She smiled a little wider. "That's better! Now put your feet up, and we'll look after you for a change."

As her friends fussed over her, their kindness made Felicity realise something.

"It's who you are that matters," she thought, "not your name!"

And knowing this made her smile one of her most dazzling and beautiful smiles ever.

The Daisy Ring

Mr Trimble loved neatness, especially in his garden. He had wonderful displays of flowers, with not a weed or bug in sight. But his pride and joy was his lawn: it was immaculate.

One morning, Mr Trimble looked out of his bedroom window and gasped. There was a ring of daisies in the middle of his beautiful lawn!

He ran to fetch his lawnmower straight away and mowed right over the daisies. "That'll fix 'em!" he said.

But the very next morning the daisy ring was back!

Over the next few weeks, Mr Trimble tried every which way to get rid of that daisy ring, but each morning it had grown back, and seemed to be looking bigger and stronger.

Mr Trimble was so frustrated he decided he would rather have no lawn at all than one spoiled by daisies. So he laid paving stones over it and made it into a patio.

That night, he was woken up by the sound of hammers on stone. He went to the window and saw an astonishing sight.

There, in the middle of his patio, was a group of tiny people attacking it with pickaxes.

Mr Trimble threw on his dressing-gown and stormed out into the garden.

"Stop! You're ruining my new patio!" he yelled.

A tiny little fellow, no bigger than Mr Trimble's foot, stood looking very cross indeed.

"Never mind your patio!" he said. "Our daisy ring can't push through all these stones!"

"But that's the point!" growled Mr Trimble.

"So that's the thanks we get!" the little man screeched. "Who do you think makes your grass so green, your plants grow so well and keeps away all the slugs and caterpillars?"

"Er… *I* do, I think!"

"You silly great oaf, we do! But if there's no fairy ring, we can't come."

"Gosh, I had no idea!" gasped Mr Trimble. "I'll get rid of the paving stones at once." And he did.

In time Mr Trimble even grew to love the daisy ring. It did look quite pretty in the middle of his immaculate lawn after all!

Playing Wizards

Harry's uncle was a wizard. He could cast all sorts of spells and was always happy to show Harry and his friends some magic. He made his spells look so easy, which set Harry's friend Sam thinking.

"I'm sure we could do one little spell," Sam pleaded.

"But *we're* not wizards," Harry insisted. "We can't do magic."

"I bet we could if we tried," said Sam. "Ask your uncle to show us."

Sam went on so much that the next time they visited Harry's uncle, Harry asked if he could turn his canary, Buttercup, into a vulture and back again. Of course, they didn't tell him they wanted to try it themselves!

They watched very carefully, noting down all the ingredients and the magic words Harry's uncle muttered as he daubed the mixture over the canary's feathers.

In a flash Buttercup changed into a large vulture with a rather grumpy expression.

Then they paid very careful attention as he reversed the spell.

The next day, Harry and Sam met in Harry's den at the bottom of the garden. Sam brought his hamster, Squeak, because neither of them had a canary to practise with.

Harry looked at the piece of paper on which he had scribbled down the ingredients for the spell. Some of them were too difficult to find – Amazonian creeper leaves, for instance – so he made do with the next best thing he could find in the garden.

"I expect they'll work," said Harry, confidently adding leaves from the creeper on the side of the house.

Harry stirred the mixture, muttering the words he'd heard his uncle use. Then he dabbed it on Squeak.

The hamster began to grow larger and larger and larger.

"It's working!" cried Harry.

Before their eyes Squeak's cute pink nose stretched into a long grey trunk, and his twitchy little ears became huge and flappy.

"Help!" gasped Harry. "He's not changing into a vulture at all! It's *much* too big. I think it's going to be … an elephant!"

Realising that they were in trouble, the boys opened the door and backed out of the den.

Before Harry could reverse the spell, Squeak the elephant trod in the bowl containing the spell mixture, then gave an enormous trumpeting cry and charged out of the den and up the path towards the house.

"Stop him!" yelled Harry, as the two boys rushed after the runaway elephant.

Luckily, Harry's uncle had a sixth sense for trouble and was on his way over to Harry's house just as Squeak came charging up the path.

He wasn't at all surprised when the elephant arrived at the front door. With a wave of his hands and a few magic words, Harry's uncle restored Squeak to his former hamster self.

"Never mess around with spells," he told Harry and Sam firmly. "If you can't get a spell absolutely right, just don't try it at all."

And Squeak was very relieved when the boys promised that this would be their last magic spell.

The Witch Trap

There was once a very unpleasant witch called Dreadnought, who spent all her time adding more and more horrible spells to her great leather-bound book of magic.

She had spells to change dogs into centipedes, or a delicious beef stew into a mouldy mess.

"We have to do something to stop her from making our lives a misery," said Mayor Nettletwist, whose shiny new limousine had just been turned into a rickety, rusty go-kart.

All the citizens of the town agreed. They had all suffered from the witch's nasty spells. But what could they do?

The mayor had a plan. "Why don't we burn her horrible spell book," he said, "and at the same time, give her a fright she'll never forget."

As it happened, every Monday morning, Witch Dreadnought walked across the fields to Chestnut Wood to collect ingredients for her spells: dead flies, smelly toadstools and whatever other gruesome things that took her fancy. She always took the same route.

One particular Monday, she was making her way to the wood as usual, when there was a loud *crack!* and a *crash!* – and the witch fell into a deep hole that had been hidden under branches and leaves.

As she tumbled into the hole, her spell book flew out of her hand and landed on the ground nearby, so she could not magic herself out of the trap.

All the townsfolk hurried across the field to see the horrible old witch ranting and raving in the hole.

"Let me out, or I'll turn you all into toads. I'll…"

"Oh, no you won't," said the mayor. "You can't because we've got your spell book!"

Mr Chop, the butcher, held the book over the hole for her to see.

The witch was furious, but there was nothing she could do. There was no danger that the villagers would use the book – they didn't know how to work spells – but that still didn't help her get out of the hole.

She sat crouched in the darkness, wondering what was going on. They were up to something, she was sure. She could hear laughter and she could smell … smoke!

Oh no! They were lighting a fire!

"Are you ready for your punishment, Witch Dreadnought?" asked the mayor.

Witch Dreadnought was aghast. Whatever were they going to do next?

"It's burning! It's burning!" cried someone, and then Witch Dreadnought realised it was her precious spell book on the fire!

But the mayor was not such an unkind man: in truth he felt sorry for the witch. Without her magic she was just a lonely old lady. "Will you promise never to have another spell book?" he asked Witch Dreadnought.

"No!" she cried. "A witch must have a spell book!"

"Very well, then," said the mayor. "But what about one with only helpful spells?"

"What fun would that be?" thought the witch.

Then she smelled the burnt leather of her book and thought of what might happen if she didn't agree. They might leave her in the hole for ever! "Very well," she said. "I promise."

So the mayor and the townsfolk helped her climb out of the hole.

Witch Dreadnought started a new spell book. It contained recipes for healing potions and creams, and spells for mending things and making them beautiful.

She soon began to make friends and found that she enjoyed helping people after all. And in time she became known far and wide as Good Witch Cure-All.

The Travelling Witch

Wanda Witch flung her cloak round her, rammed her hat onto her head and, calling her cat, ran out into her back yard to collect her broomstick. She sat astride it with Blackberry, her cat, perched behind, and commanded her broom to take them to Wickity Hill. But the broomstick didn't so much as twitch a twig.

Wanda shook it angrily.

"Come on, let's get going!" she screeched. "We'll be late for the coven!"

But no matter what she did, the broomstick would not budge.

"The magic must have worn out!" Wanda stamped her foot. "Well, there's no time to work a revival spell now. What am I going to do, Blackberry? I can't miss the meeting – we're choosing a new Chief Witch!"

"You could go by train," said Blackberry.

By train? Now there was a thought. It would ruin her image as a witch, of course, but Wanda didn't have much choice. Her broom was well and truly useless.

She put Blackberry into his travel basket and ran down to the railway station.

She rushed through the entrance and marched into the ticket office. "A return ticket to Wickity Hill!" she snapped rudely at the man behind the counter. "And make it quick – I'm running late!"

"I've never heard of that station. You'd better ask the ticket collector," he replied, looking doubtfully at Wanda. "Are you off to a fancy dress party?"

"Of course not!" spluttered Wanda. She could hear a train approaching. "Surely *you* must have heard of Wickity Hill!" she demanded of the ticket collector, as she barged in front of another lady who was waiting.

Fortunately, he knew it and told Wanda the best station to get off at. Not stopping to thank him, Wanda sped onto the platform.

"Meeeoww!" wailed Blackberry from his basket, realising he was about to be left behind. But Wanda didn't hear him. She flung open the door of a carriage and leaped on, just as a sudden gust of wind sent her pointed hat tumbling away along the platform.

"My hat!" wailed Wanda, as the train pulled out of the station.

Before long, Wanda saw the familiar shape of Wickity Hill ahead. The coven was just beginning as Wanda dashed up the hill. All the witches were already gathered round, each with their own black cat.

The Chief Witch frowned as Wanda arrived, hatless, catless and without her broomstick.

"Who are you?" she asked. "An outsider? Away with you! This is a coven – it's for witches only!"

"But it's me, Wanda Witch!" said Wanda.

"Nonsense!" cried the Chief Witch. "Wanda Witch has a broomstick, a black cat and a tall hat. *You* have none of these things."

Wanda tried to tell them what had happened, but they wouldn't listen. The witches all shooed her away with their broomsticks, convinced she was an impostor.

Wanda Witch fled.

She had a long wait for the next train home, and when she got there she found Blackberry sitting on the station bench, being looked after by the ticket collector.

"I'm staying here," he purred. "I'm fed up with being a grumpy witch's cat. I'm going to be a station cat instead."

So Wanda Witch returned home to her cottage without her cat and without her hat. The Chief Witch had said she couldn't be a witch without these things. Well, perhaps she wouldn't be a witch any more. Perhaps she would be happier not being a witch at all.

Wanda Witch felt a whole new life was just beginning!

The Spelling Book

Jenny was feeling sorry for herself. She'd only got two of her spellings right at school that day and she was beginning to despair of ever getting better at it.

It was just then that she spotted a book stall at the market – which was strange, as there wasn't usually. In the middle of the stall was a book with SPELLING BOOK printed in bold black letters on the worn red leather cover.

She bought it, hoping it would contain lists of words which she could practise and learn to spell. But when she got home and opened it, there were no words at all, just funny-looking squiggles and numbers!

"What's the use of a spelling book if I can't even read it?" she sighed. But as she closed the book, she noticed a label just inside the front cover, and written on the label in spidery purple handwriting it said:

Property of W. Merlin, 9 Lancelot Court, Tintagel.

This puzzled Jenny. Why would someone leave their name and address in a book that they were giving away, she wondered?

Now, Tintagel happened to be not far from Jenny's home, and after tea Jenny asked her Mum if they might see if they could find the original owner of the book, and return it to him.

Fortunately Jenny's Mum agreed, and together they took the book round to the address on the label. The front door had a funny brass knocker on it shaped like a dragon. Jenny thought she saw the dragon wink at her as she knocked, and she felt just a little bit afraid.

A rather strange-looking man opened the door. He was tall and thin, with a long white beard and big bushy eyebrows over piercing blue eyes.

"Er, are you Mr Merlin?" asked Jenny. "We've brought your spelling book back."

The old man's face lit up. "You've found it! Thank goodness! I can't do my job without it."

Jenny suddenly realised what the book really was. "It's for *magic* spells, isn't it?" she said.

"It is indeed," smiled Mr Merlin, gratefully taking the book from her. "It contains every magic spell I could ever need. I'm a wizard, you see. Do come in! You must have a reward for returning my precious book."

Jenny and her mum followed Mr Merlin into the house. An owl was asleep on a perch in the corner.

"Now, what would you like best in all the world?" asked Mr Merlin. "I can make anything happen for you, anything at all."

It was tempting to ask for a pony, or lots of money and a palace to live in, but Jenny remembered from her storybooks that wishes like those hardly ever worked out well.

Then she thought of something that would be far more useful to her.

"I'd like to be able to spell," she said. "Words, that is, not doing magic."

Mr Merlin nodded approvingly. "Oh, that's a very fine wish!" he said. He opened his book, found a page and muttered a few strange words. A wisp of purple smoke curled around Jenny's head.

"There! Now you'll be the very best speller in the land!" he told her.

But what Mr Merlin didn't say was that the spell would only last one month. That didn't worry Jenny, though. After a month of coming top of the class, she was so confident and determined that she always learned her spellings from then on!

Fairy Cakes

Jiminy Goblin was passing the baker's shop one day when he saw some little cakes in the window. He went inside and asked the baker what they were.

"Why, they're fairy cakes, of course," the baker replied.

They looked delicious: two thin slices of cake stood upright in each little paper case, like little fairy wings, with delicious butter cream in the middle and colourful sprinkles on top. Jiminy couldn't resist.

"I'll take a dozen!" he said.

But later, as he was preparing his tea, his mouth watering at the thought of the little cakes waiting to be eaten, a thought occurred to him.

"Fairy cakes… Does that mean they are enchanted? Will I change into something horrible if I eat them? Perhaps I'll change into a fairy." Jiminy shuddered at the thought. But it gave him an idea.

He decided not to eat the fairy cakes after all, but to make some of his own. "I'll call them goblin cakes," he chuckled. "And I'll put my own special spell in them that will turn whoever eats them into my servant! Ha ha!"

40

Jiminy made the goblin cakes and invited three of his goblin friends round to tea.

"Do have a cake," he told them.

"Yum-yum. These are delicious, Jiminy," said Lennie Loafer, as he greedily reached for another.

The plate of cakes soon disappeared. Within minutes Jiminy's spell had began to work and he had three new helpers running around, doing all the jobs he hated doing himself. They grumbled of course, but because of the spell they could not stop – and there was plenty to do because Jiminy was so untidy.

Meanwhile, Jiminy went into the garden and stretched out in the sun. "This is the life!" he thought to himself.

A short time later a young man who looked like a traveller – but who happened to be a wizard – stopped by his gate.

"Hello there!" said the man. "Could you spare a traveller a cup of tea?"

"Certainly," said Jiminy, and he called towards the house. "The gentleman here wants a drink! And give him one of my cakes as well."

"A cake!" said the young man in surprise. "Why, that's very kind of you!" He picked up the cake and studied it. "Hmm," he said thoughtfully as he looked through the cottage window. "I think you're trying to put me under a spell, like those goblins in there."

"Me?" said Jiminy, feigning surprise. "A spell?"

"Well, if you're not, then prove it. Take a bite of the cake yourself," said the young man. "A big bite."

"Glad to," said Jiminy, for he knew his spell would only affect other people. He took a mouthful of cake. The young man suddenly made a strange movement with his hand. He then turned towards the gate and beckoned to Jiminy, who found himself following, even though he didn't want to.

"Silly goblin," said the young man. "Now you are my servant, for I have turned your spell back on itself."

Jiminy Goblin had to follow the wizard and do everything he was told. His three friends worked hard in the cottage until their spells wore off. But poor Jiminy is still the wizard's servant to this very day.

The Halloween Party

"Listen, class," said Miss Fox. "Next Tuesday is Hallowe'en, and the school is going to have a big party with lots of games!"

"Everyone should dress up," Miss Fox continued, "and I'd like you each to bring some spooky things for us all to eat. Sausage broomsticks, for instance, or oranges carved with funny faces."

All the children were excited, except Lizzie Wimple. She told Miss Fox she was too busy to come.

"Too busy for a Hallowe'en party?" asked Miss Fox.

"Well, err… The thing is, Hallowe'en is always a very busy time at home," Lizzie explained.

As soon as she got home, Lizzie told her mum about the party. "It will just be silly," she said. "Everyone dressing up in costumes, and no *real* magic at all."

Lizzie's mother smiled. "Well, perhaps we could do something about that," she said with a wink.

"But I said I wasn't going," said Lizzie.

"Think about it. You could do something special to surprise them all!" Lizzie's mum was one of those good witches who used magic for fun as well as serious things.

"All right," said Lizzie. "But could we bake a special cake, please?"

Hallowe'en came. By six o'clock, all the children had arrived – dressed up as ghosts, witches, skeletons, vampires and other incredible monsters. There was lots of delicious food too. And, of course, the cake baked by Lizzie's mum, with black icing and sparkly orange stars.

"It's time to light the lanterns," said Miss Fox. They all went out into the playground, where the pumpkin lanterns that the children had carved earlier in the week were all lined up. Their flickering candles made the playground look spooky and mysterious.

But then, just as the children were about to go back inside to play games, they heard a strange swooshing sound in the air. They looked up – and saw Lizzie Wimple dressed as a witch, flying across the playing fields towards them on a broomstick.

"Wow!" said Jack. "How does she do that?"

"It must be magic!" gasped Kate.

Lizzie flew once round the playground, did a loop-the-loop, then landed expertly. Everyone crowded round, admiring the broom and all wishing they could have a go.

But the most magical part of the evening came when the mysterious black cake was cut. Lizzie's friend Jack was the first to try it. If he hadn't believed in magic before, he certainly did now. The cake tasted of all his favourite foods, all at once!

When he'd finished it, he felt he wanted to rush into the playground and take to the air, just like Lizzie.

And that's just what he did – without even a broomstick or a pair of wings!

Soon everyone had eaten some of the magical cake and the air was filled with flying children and teachers!

They all agreed that it was truly the most wonderful Hallowe'en party ever.

"Well," said Lizzie to herself, "I always knew Mum baked light cakes, but she must have used masses of magical self-raising flour for this one!"

The New Broom

Hattie Hickory lived in a crooked old cottage with cobwebs in every corner. Dusty old books of spells spilled from shelves and covered every inch of spare floor space. The cupboards were stuffed with potion bottles, and bunches of dried herbs hung from every beam. It was all very untidy, but that's just how Hattie liked it.

But one day Hattie Hickory tripped over a pile of books and spilled a whole bottle of wart cure over her best broomstick. Immediately, the bristles shrivelled and fell off the stick.

"Bother!" she cried. "Now I need a new broom."

"What you need," said her cat, Spitfire, "is a helper."

"Good idea! I'll advertise for one," said Hattie.

A week later, Daphne Doogood arrived. She was a neat lady with a brisk, cheerful manner. She wasn't quite the sort of person Hattie had in mind. She would have preferred someone she could boss about, but Daphne would have to do, as nobody else had applied for the job.

"I'm off into town to buy a new broomstick," Hattie told Daphne on her first morning. "While I'm out, please tidy the spell books and arrange all the potions in alphabetical order, so that I can find them easily."

Daphne Doogood was delighted. She loved tidying up and organising things.

Hattie Hickory's shopping trip took rather longer than she expected. She was very particular when it came to broomsticks, and she was determined to find exactly the right one. When at last she arrived back home, she wondered if she'd come to the right place.

The cottage windows were wide open. Freshly-washed curtains were drying on the line. When Hattie pushed the cottage door open she smelled a most unfamiliar smell – disinfectant and furniture polish!

Her living room was unrecognisable. It was clean and bright, with not a cobweb in sight. The furniture gleamed and a vase of fresh flowers stood on the table.

Not even Spitfire had escaped. He cowered under the table, his fur washed and brushed and a new velvet collar round his neck.

Daphne Doogood was just tipping Hattie's collection of stuffed toads into the dustbin.

"What on earth have you done?" gasped Hattie.

Daphne beamed at her. "Doesn't it look lovely? Oh, and I've cleared out all those dusty old books onto a bonfire."

"Oh, no!" Hattie Hickory felt faint. She dashed into the back garden. It was true! A bonfire was burning merrily, and she could see the remains of her spell books crackling and sparking as they crumbled into ashes.

Turning to Daphne, who was busily trimming the grass, Hattie Hickory spluttered furiously.

"I'll turn you into a rat! I'll give you purple boils…"

But, of course, she could do none of these things without her spell books!

Spitfire grinned down from the top of the garden wall. "Meow! They do say that a new broom sweeps clean," he said with a grin, "but I don't think Hattie wanted her home quite *this* clean!"

Nat's Magic Seedling

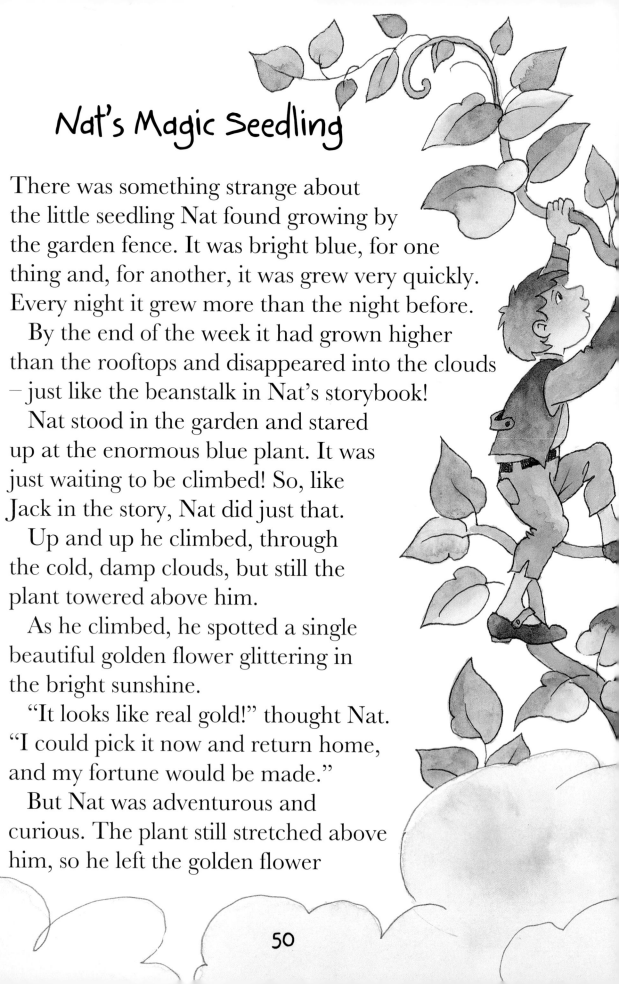

There was something strange about the little seedling Nat found growing by the garden fence. It was bright blue, for one thing and, for another, it was grew very quickly. Every night it grew more than the night before.

By the end of the week it had grown higher than the rooftops and disappeared into the clouds – just like the beanstalk in Nat's storybook!

Nat stood in the garden and stared up at the enormous blue plant. It was just waiting to be climbed! So, like Jack in the story, Nat did just that.

Up and up he climbed, through the cold, damp clouds, but still the plant towered above him.

As he climbed, he spotted a single beautiful golden flower glittering in the bright sunshine.

"It looks like real gold!" thought Nat. "I could pick it now and return home, and my fortune would be made."

But Nat was adventurous and curious. The plant still stretched above him, so he left the golden flower

and climbed on until he finally arrived at the top of the plant.

He was not at all surprised when he found that he could step onto the clouds that had gathered around it. Nat half expected to see a giant's castle, but something quite different came out of the mist.

It was a wizard. He wore a splendid cloak of midnight blue with golden stars, and a tall, black conical hat.

They stared at each other.

"Have you anything in your pocket?" demanded the wizard.

"N-not much," Nat replied nervously, remembering how he had nearly been tempted to pick the golden flower. He pulled out a dirty handkerchief, a corkscrew and a whistle.

"No golden flowers?" asked the wizard.

Nat shook his head.

51

To his surprise, the wizard laughed delightedly.

"Splendid!" he said. "That's why you are the only person ever to have reached the top of the plant. Everyone else who climbed it stopped to pick a golden flower and took it home. Much good it did them, for as soon as they put their feet on the ground, it turned to dust! Now at last I've met someone whose curiosity is greater than their greed."

The wizard took a small wooden box from his pocket and presented it to Nat.

"Inside this box is a seed. Plant it carefully and look after it well, and it will soon grow as tall as a sunflower. Don't give it any water. Clean the leaves every day with metal polish, and sing it a lullaby each night."

Nat was rather puzzled, but thanked the wizard and waved goodbye. He climbed back down the plant and did exactly as the wizard instructed. Before long, a small blue shoot appeared. And by the end of the summer, Nat had picked a whole bunch of beautiful flowers, every one of which was made of purest gold.

The Broomstick Race

Mr Toopuddle specialised in making broomsticks for witches. But it didn't make him much money because he didn't sell very many. Witches were becoming rarer and rarer, and those that were still around seldom bought new brooms. Things were getting rather desperate for poor Mr Toopuddle. He started to wonder how he could continue to make a living.

Then one day he had a bright idea: he would organise a broomstick race, and the prize would be a special luxury broom.

It took him many days to complete, but the prize broom was his very finest creation: it had a polished wooden handle, carved at the top into the shape of a cat's head, and beautifully-laid oiled willow twigs. He placed it in the window of his shop, together with a poster giving details of the race.

Before long, every witch in the land had heard about the race – and the wonderful broomstick that would go to the winner – and they were queuing to sign up to take part.

The day of the race was overcast and windy. The competitors set off eagerly on their splintered old broomsticks, but some didn't even make it beyond Nightshade Woods before their broomsticks fell apart! Others lost their way among the heavy clouds. And some were simply blown off their brooms. Only three made it to the finishing line outside Mr Toopuddle's shop, and the winner was Witch Hellebore.

She accepted the prize broomstick with glee, knowing she would be the envy of every witch in the land.

The other witches looked gloomily at their tired old broomsticks.

"I want one just like that!" wailed Witch Muckleberry.

"So do I!" shouted Witch Batswing.

"I'd be delighted to make one for each of you," smiled Mr Toopuddle.

The two witches considered his offer. They'd have to pay for them, of course, but it would be worth it to have new brooms just like Witch Hellebore's.

Mr Toopuddle's plan worked better than he had dreamed. None of the witches wanted to be outdone by her sisters. Before long, every witch from far and wide had ordered a deluxe new broomstick. Mr Toopuddle made such a fortune that he never had to work again!

The Magic Bicycle

The bicycle Ellie received on her eighth birthday looked perfectly ordinary. It was black and gold with a shiny silver bell. At first she had been very disappointed because she hadn't really wanted a bicycle at all – she was desperate to get a pony! But when Ellie looked at the bicycle more closely, she found a little cluster of golden stars just under the saddle. She felt they made it rather special.

Ellie asked her mum where she had bought it.

"That funny little shop in the village," her mum replied.

Ellie knew the shop. It was full of old and dusty second-hand bicycles that made hers look very smart by comparison.

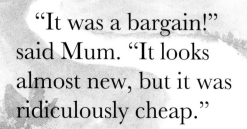

"It was a bargain!" said Mum. "It looks almost new, but it was ridiculously cheap."

"Hmmm," thought Ellie. "That's odd." But she couldn't wait to try it out. She decided to ride down the hill to the village on it.

So she popped on her helmet and set off for Steeplechase Hill.

The hill was very steep, with a sharp bend at the bottom. As Ellie went whizzing down it at top speed, she squeezed on the brake handles – but nothing happened! Faster and faster went the bike, with Ellie hanging on with gritted teeth.

When they reached the bottom, something extraordinary happened: the bicycle gave a little buck – and jumped right across the bend to where the road straightened out again!

"Wow!" thought Ellie. "That was neat!"

She patted the bike absentmindedly as though it were a pony. It certainly seemed to act like one. As she rode down towards the village it kept giving excited little bucks and tossing its handlebars. She even thought she could hear it whinnying.

Back home, Ellie looked again at the little stars under the saddle and saw they were in a horseshoe shape. She hadn't noticed that before. "I bet I'm the only person in the world with a pony-cycle!" she thought.

Ellie took her bicycle out for a ride every day. Sometimes they cantered across the fields and even jumped the hedges. She was sure that if she treated her bicycle just like a pony, one day it might turn into one.

And would you believe, Ellie was seen riding a little bay pony in the village just last week – so perhaps it did!

The Monster Under the Pavement

Kerry saw monsters everywhere: in the linen cupboard, under the bed, and even behind her wardrobe.

"There are no such things as monsters," her mum said the day Kerry ran in to tell her that the linen cupboard monster was curled up on top of the spare duvet. "It's probably the cat."

But Kerry knew better.

Then one morning, as Kerry and her mum were waiting at the bus stop to go to the shops, a pair of skinny arms poked up from a manhole in the pavement and grabbed Kerry's ankles.

"Mum, help!" screamed Kerry. "A monster's got me!"

"Don't be silly, dear," said Kerry's mum absentmindedly. She was busy studying her shopping list and didn't notice Kerry being dragged out of sight behind her.

Kerry dropped into the hole and landed with a splash in a cold underground stream. Then something pulled her from the water and placed her on a narrow ledge.

Kerry opened her eyes. She saw a small monster with three eyes, fluffy black fur and huge pink ears.

"What do you want?" asked Kerry, nervously.

"I want my friends back," said the monster.

"Well, what can I do about it?"

"They're trapped behind your wardrobe, under your bed, and in your linen cupboard," replied the monster. "Didn't you see them?"

Kerry told him her mum said she was just seeing things – but now she knew the monsters were real.

"You just need to set them free," said the monster. "Then lift up this manhole cover so they can come home."

It didn't sound too difficult, Kerry thought.

The monster took Kerry's hand and helped her back up the long ladder to the surface again.

"Goodbye," he said. "Don't forget, now!"

As if she could!

Mum was still standing on the pavement, trying to work out if she'd written "potatoes" or "tomatoes", as Kerry climbed back out of the manhole.

"Hi, Mum!"

"Oh, there you are, dear," said Mum. "I thought you'd gone home again."

"Um… if you don't mind, I think I will," said Kerry. "I have something important to do."

"All right, dear," said Mum.

Kerry ran back home and rang the doorbell.

"I'm just baking a cake," said Gran cheerfully, when she opened the door.

"I'll keep out of your way!" said Kerry as she ran straight upstairs, relieved that the coast was clear.

She went first to the linen cupboard. The monster was caught up in a sheet, so Kerry untangled him. "Come with me," whispered Kerry, "but be very quiet!"

In her bedroom, the under-the-bed monster was stuck to the floor by a sticky old toffee. Kerry gently prised him free.

The monster behind the wardrobe had its fur caught on a nail. Kerry snipped it free with her scissors.

"Come on, quickly!" she said to the three monsters, and they scuttled after her, down the stairs, out of the door, and along the street to the manhole.

Kerry struggled to lift the cover, but the moment she did, the monsters wasted no time in jumping down into the black hole. She heard three splashes as they landed at the bottom, and very faintly she heard a distant cheer as they were welcomed home again.

The Magic Stone

One day, a stone caught Jason's eye in the park and he picked it up.

"What's so special about that?" said Evie, as she looked at the large grey pebble in her brother's hand.

"But it's completely round – just like a ball," Jason protested.

"Oh, just get rid of it," Evie told him. "You've enough junk as it is."

But Jason was convinced there was something special about the stone, and he stuffed it in his pocket for later.

That night, just as he was drifting off to sleep, Jason became aware of a strange light filling his bedroom. It seemed to be coming from his jeans on the back of his chair. Then he remembered the stone!

He jumped out of bed, and took the stone out from his jeans pocket.

It shone so brightly that Jason gasped.

What could it be?

Then, suddenly, the light faded and the stone became plain grey once more. Jason's room was in darkness again. He went over to the window and pulled the curtains open. Thick clouds covered the Moon.

"I wonder if the stone reacts to moonlight?" he thought. He decided to wake Evie up to ask her. Perhaps she could work it out.

Evie shuffled into his room, her eyes heavy with sleep. She didn't believe what Jason was telling her.

"Are you mad?" she grumbled. "Did you wake me up just to show me your silly stone?"

Jason's eyes began to fill with tears. It was horrible not to be believed. But just as Evie turned to go back to her own room, the Moon came out from behind the clouds, and the stone blazed into life again.

"Wow!" gasped Evie.

"It's weird … magical!" said Jason, feeling uneasy. "I think we'd better put the stone back where we found it. It might belong to somebody, or something."

"How can we?" asked Evie. "We'd wake the whole neighbourhood with that bright light."

As they were standing there, puzzling about what to do, something else quite extraordinary happened.

"Look at the Moon, Evie!" cried Jason.

The huge, round shape of the Moon suddenly filled the window. Enormous sad eyes seemed to stare at them, peering into the room.

Evie shuddered a little. "It looks as if it is searching for something!"

Jason knew just what to do. As quietly as he could, he opened the window and placed the stone on the windowsill outside.

The Moon was now so close they could almost touch it. Its huge face seemed to absorb the light of the stone. As the children watched, the two flared into a single dazzling light that blazed so brightly they had to turn their faces away.

When they looked back, the stone was gone and the Moon was back in its proper place in the night sky, but rather than the mournful face they'd seen before, they felt sure that it was now smiling.

Cat on a Broomstick

Life as a witch's cat didn't suit Jetstone at all.

When he first arrived at Witch Humpledink's cottage, it had all looked very promising. There was a cosy sitting room with a fireside rug where he settled himself comfortably. But as night fell, Witch Humpledink threw on her cloak and perched Jetstone on her broomstick.

How Jetstone came to hate that broomstick! He dreaded the freezing night flights, with the wind chilling his whiskers. His mistress never seemed to notice her cat's discomfort. The worse the weather, the better she liked it. And to make matters worse he was scared of heights!

But Jetstone didn't dare complain in case she turned him into something horrid.

One particularly foul evening, when the rain was beating against the cottage windows, Jetstone decided he had had enough. "I don't want to be a witch's cat any more," he said to himself. "I want a nice warm farmhouse kitchen where I can catch mice, and not have to spend my nights flying over the rooftops!"

"Here, Jetstone!" called Witch Humpledink. "It's time to go out."

Jetstone pretended not to hear. "JETSTONE!" roared the witch. "Come here AT ONCE!"

Jetstone reluctantly got to his feet and stretched, then padded after her to the door.

Witch Humpledink picked him up and deposited him on the broomstick. He clung on tight as it shot into the air and swooped giddily across to the wood.

Jetstone looked down at the carpet of leaves rushing past below. It was now or never! He took a deep breath, closed his eyes, and then he jumped.

It was a long way to the ground! But Jetstone landed the right way up, on all four feet – as cats do – and waited as the broomstick flew on out of sight. Then he ran through the wood until he came to a farmyard. He dived into the barn, shook off some of the rain and settled down to sleep in the hay. In the morning he was woken by voices.

"Look! A black cat!"

"Is it a stray?"

"He looks like Witch Humpledink's cat."

Jetstone opened his eyes to find the farmer, his wife and their little daughter all looking down at him.

"No, he can't be the witch's cat," said the farmer's wife. "Look – he has white whiskers. Witch Humpledink's cat is completely black."

White whiskers? Jetstone squinted down at them, and saw that they were indeed snowy white. He remembered jumping off the broomstick and running through the wood. Perhaps his whiskers had turned white with fright. But whatever the reason, at least his days as a witch's cat were over!

"Let's take him indoors," said the farmer. "He looks so cold and hungry."

Jetstone curled up in front of the warm kitchen stove, purring contentedly, happy that he'd taken his last ever broomstick ride!

Dragon Fire

At one time, dragons didn't breathe fire, so it was quite safe for them to live in houses.

Like all dragons, Clarence loved to be warm. He was happiest curled up and snoozing by a roaring fire in his cosy little house – but sometimes he had to go out, and then he always felt the cold.

One winter's day, Clarence was flying home when it started to snow. A snowflake plopped on to his nose.

"Brrr!" he shivered. "I wish I could carry my nice warm fire around with me, then I'd never feel cold again!"

He thought his idea
was such a good one
that he turned around
and flew to the cottage
where the wizard lived.

"Hmm," the wizard
frowned as Clarence
explained what he
wanted. "Fire spells
can easily get out of hand, you know."

But Clarence pleaded so pitifully that the wizard
finally took down his thick leather-bound spell book and
leafed through the pages.

"Ah, here we are," he said. He read the spell carefully,
collected the ingredients and then stirred them into
his big copper pot until they became a thick, brown,
horrible-smelling brew. The potion was ready.

"Open wide," said the wizard. Clarence swallowed
the mixture and immediately he began to feel very hot.
The spell was working!

He thanked the wizard and gave him five pieces of
precious dragon gold.

Outside in the snowy street, Clarence began to wonder if he'd parted with his gold a little too soon. There was no sign of any fire around him that he could see. Although his insides were hot, the outside was as cold as ever, and he couldn't wait to warm up.

Just as he arrived at his front door, he felt a sneeze coming on. "Atish-atish-ATISHOOOOO! Oh, help!"

For as Clarence had opened his mouth to sneeze, a huge flame shot out of his mouth and scorched his front door. He sneezed again as he went into the kitchen and this time he set fire to the curtains.

In a very short time, Clarence's lovely little home had burnt to cinders. So much for carrying his fire around with him!

Clarence now had to find a new home that wouldn't catch fire every time he sneezed. He flew up into the hills and found a big, deep cave. He lit a bonfire in front of it, then fell fast asleep.

As it turned out, Clarence was very
pleased with his new home. His friends were
impressed, too. They thought it was a
very fine place for a dragon to live
– and very low-maintenance!
Also, breathing fire was a jolly
useful thing to be able to do too.

One by one they all visited the wizard for their own
fire spells. And that's how it was that dragons came to
live in caves and breathe fire.

The Little Yellow Goblin

Once upon a time, a little yellow goblin lived under a big stone in Nightingale Lane. He was an ugly fellow and fond of mean tricks. If a horse was passing by, he would leap out and frighten it, so that it bolted with its rider. And he would kick children on the ankle if they came near his stone. But no one ever saw him.

No one except Sophie, that is. The goblin had just bitten Sophie's friend Bella on the leg. While Bella yelped and hopped about, Sophie looked around to see what had bitten her. She didn't have to look far: she soon spotted the small, mean-looking yellow goblin peeking from behind the stone. "Hey!" cried Sophie. "Why did you just bite my friend?"

The goblin tried to run away and hide, but Sophie caught him by the scruff of his neck and held on tight as he struggled and squirmed.

"I asked you a question," she said.

"I heard you," grumbled the goblin. "Let me go and I'll tell you."

"Oh no," said Sophie. "I know all about your goblin tricks! I've a good mind to put you in a jar and take you to Witch Hazel to see if she'd like to keep you as a pet."

"Please, no!" squealed the goblin. "I don't want to live in a jar forever!"

"I'm sure Bella – and all the other people you've hurt – wouldn't mind."

"But playing tricks is the only way I get noticed," muttered the goblin, sulkily. "I'm so small that no one ever sees me."

"You don't have to be nasty to be noticed," said Sophie. "Try being nice, instead!"

"But it's much more fun being nasty."

"Really?" asked Sophie. "Let's go, then!"

"All right!" cried the goblin, frantically. "I'll be nice, I promise!"

"I bet he doesn't keep his promises," said Bella.

"Goblin's word," said the goblin solemnly.

Sophie let him go. "We'll know where to find you again if you don't," she warned.

Soon after, strange things started happening in Nightingale Lane. An old lady found a beautiful bunch of daffodils in her basket. And a lost traveller was helped on his way by a funny little yellow man.

The next time Sophie and Bella walked along Nightingale Lane they met a pleasant-faced young man.

"Wow! You've grown!" said Sophie in amazement, looking at the goblin that she'd last seen living under a stone.

"Every time I do a good deed, I grow a bit taller," said the goblin. "It feels wonderful!"

"I'm glad to hear it," said Sophie, as she shook his hand. "But don't stop being good once you've grown as tall as you want to be, will you?"

"I won't," smiled the goblin. "Goblin's word!"

The Troll in the Pool

In the middle of a dark wood was a deep and murky pool, and in the middle of the pool, there lived a troll. Everyone knew it was there. They'd seen its moon-eyes looking up at them from the water, or spotted a scaly claw reaching out as they passed by.

And everyone knew that the troll ate people. It was said that the woodcutter's great-great-great grandfather had been gobbled up whole, and it was believed to be particularly fond of naughty children!

Most people avoided the wood, but not Marcus Goodheart. He was a soldier travelling back home from his barrracks to see his family again. He was anxious to get home as soon as possible and the shortcut through the wood was the quickest way by far.

He marched along at a brisk pace, singing as he went. Being a brave and fearless soldier, he wasn't worried about a little thing like a troll, so he stopped by the pool to rest. "It's just a silly tale," he thought.

Then, deep down in the pool, something stirred.

Before he could flee, a huge shape rose from the water and a slimy claw grabbed his leg. He shook it, trying to wriggle free, but then the rest of the troll emerged. It was a horrible muddy-green colour and very, very ugly.

"Let go of me!" demanded Marcus.

"No, please stay!" cried the troll.

"You can talk!" said Marcus in amazement.

"Of course I can," the troll replied. "Not that I get much chance to practise. Nobody ever comes here any more."

The troll let go of Marcus's leg and climbed out of the water and on to the bank.

"Well, I'm not surprised that no one comes near you," said Marcus, without thinking. "You're so…"

"I know," said the troll, dropping his head. "I'm ugly, that's why. All trolls are ugly. Otherwise we wouldn't be trolls." Tears welled up in his big eyes.

Although the troll had let go of his leg, Marcus no longer wanted to run away. He could see that the creature was not terrible at all, just very lonely and sad.

"I expect you'd look very handsome to another troll," said Marcus. "But people are afraid because they think you will eat them."

"Whatever gave them that idea? I'm a vegetarian. I always have been."

"What about the woodcutter's great-great-great grandfather?"

"I'm not that old, you know," said the troll. "That was my great-great grandfather, and in any case the story has been very much exaggerated. But we don't talk about him. All I want is a bit of company and a chat."

Marcus reached out and patted the troll's large, clammy hand. "I'll come and see you," he promised. "And I'll bring my family, too, so that when I go back to my regiment you'll still have visitors."

The troll's eyes glowed with gratitude.

He still lives in the pond in the middle of the wood, but now the troll has plenty of friends. All the villagers come to see him regularly and have a picnic by the pool. And of course they always remember to bring extra food for the troll, especially his favourite – strawberry buns!

All That Glitters

Barnaby Bassett and his wife, Mary, had a nice little cottage, and a fine black-and-white cow that gave them plenty of creamy milk. Yet despite their comfortable life, Barnaby was not happy. He wanted to be rich. He wished with all his heart that his cellar was full of gold.

"Even just one bag of gold would do," he said.

It's not that he wanted to spend it. He just wanted to be able to gloat over it. Barnaby Bassett had the makings of a true miser.

One day, there was a knock on their door. Barnaby opened it and he saw a little man standing on the doorstep. He was dressed all in green with a red feather in his cap. "Would you be good enough to sell me that fine cow?" asked the man.

"Sell her? But she's all we have," replied Barnaby.

"Don't even think of it," said Mary.

"She's a very fine cow," said the man with a cunning look.

"Yes," said Barnaby, suddenly having an idea. "She's worth her weight in gold."

"And it's gold I'll be giving you," said the man, bringing out a large, bulging sack from behind his back.

Barnaby's eyes grew wide.

The little man took out a handful of shiny gold coins that glittered in the sunlight. He held one out to Barnaby, who took it with trembling fingers and bit it to make sure it was real.

"All right," said Barnaby quickly, before his wife could say anything. "The cow's yours."

"Ther's no need to see me off," said the little man. "I'll lead her out myself." And with that he turned and went, leaving Barnaby with the sack of gold.

"Give me a hand, Mary," he said. "This sack will be very heavy."

Mary sighed. "I just hope you've done the right thing, I have a bad feeling about this. That little man looked like a leprechaun to me. You can't trust them – you know how mischievous they are."

She came over to the door and they each took hold of a corner of the sack and pulled.

But to their dismay, it lifted easily and weighed almost nothing at all.

With a sinking heart, Barnaby opened the sack. It was stuffed with leaves. He had been tricked!

"B-but it was real gold, truly it was!" he stammered.

"I told you!" said Mary, crossly. "But did you listen?"

They rushed to the window, but both the little man and the cow were nowhere to be seen.

"Perhaps now you'll stop dreaming of what you can't have, and work for what you can," chided Mary.

And from that day on, Barnaby worked hard until he had saved up enough money for another cow and no longer wasted time dreaming of a cellar full of gold.

Not Quite a Dragon

Rachel and Patrick found the creature one day while they were walking home from school. Patrick went to throw an empty drink can into a litter bin, when he saw the rubbish move. He let out a cry of startled surprise.

"Rachel! There's something alive in here!"

They peered into the bin. Certainly, something was moving underneath some greasy newspaper. Suddenly, a head popped out, making the children jump.

They'd never seen anything like it. It had bulging amber eyes, a long tail and little spiky wings. Its greeny-yellow skin was scaly, like a lizard's. It was about the size of a small cat and it was trying hard to scramble out of the bin.

"Wow! It looks like a dragon," gasped Patrick.

"It's too small to be a dragon," said Rachel.

The creature gave a little chirp.

"It doesn't seem to like it in the litter bin," said Patrick. "Do you think we ought to help it out?"

"Of course," said Rachel. She gripped the creature round the middle and lifted it out of the bin. It clung tightly to her, its sharp claws catching in her sweater. She carefully unhooked them and it cuddled down in her arms.

Patrick gently stroked its scaly head with his finger.

"Can we take it home with us?" he asked. But Rachel shook her head. She knew just how much Patrick wanted a pet, but it wouldn't do to keep this strange little animal.

"It would really be best to leave here," she said. "I'm sure it will probably make its own way home."

She put the creature down and she and Patrick walked away quickly. Unfortunately, the little thing seemed determined to follow them. It flapped its tiny wings and hopped awkwardly after them.

"Oh dear," said Rachel. "This isn't good…"

Just then they heard a tremendously loud wooshing noise overhead. They looked up to see a huge dragon soaring above them!

Patrick yelped and ducked, but Rachel just stood and stared.

It was the most amazing sight she had ever seen. The dragon swooped down and scooped up the tiny little creature on the pavement.

"Oh no!" said Patrick. "The big one's going to eat it!"

"No, it won't," said Rachel. "Look, she's its mother!"

Both children stared in wonder, watching the dragon and its baby fly away, until they were just a spot in the far distance and finally vanished.

Rachel put her arm round her brother. "Don't be sad, Patrick. If we hadn't pulled the little dragon out of that litter bin, its mother would never have found it."

"But I wanted to keep it," said Patrick, close to tears.

"It'll be much better off with its mother," Rachel said sensibly.

And in his heart Patrick knew his sister was right.

Witch Twinkletoes

Witch Batswing was pulling on her long black boots one day when she noticed the soles had huge holes in them.

"Not even magic will put those right," she said. "I'll have to buy a new pair." And off she flew to the shoe shop in Witch Hollow.

The shop had a great many pairs of boots on display. Fine green boots, shiny pink boots and a black pair just like her own. But the ones that Witch Batswing fancied most were silver and gold, dotted with sparkling diamonds. They were dreadfully expensive. Witch Batswing hadn't nearly enough money in her purse for them, but she felt sure that a simple magic spell would put that right…

Despite her enormous feet and huge bunions, as soon as she put them on, the boots fitted Witch Batswing perfectly.

"I'll take them!" she declared, handing the shop assistant three gold pieces and telling him to keep the change.

The assistant beamed. "Oh, thank you!" he said, bowing gratefully.

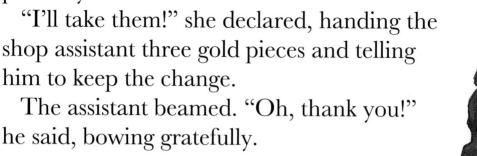

That night Witch Batswing flew to Spelltop Beacon, the meeting place of the local witches.

"Well, what do you think?" she said, as she paraded in her new boots.

"How vulgar!" said Witch Hemlock, enviously.

"Dreadful!" cried Witch Waysop.

"TAKE THEM OFF AT ONCE!" screeched the Chief Witch. "No *real* witch would wear boots like that!"

"But they make me feel so beautiful and elegant," said Witch Batswing. And it was true! She looked as radiant as a fairy princess. Her boots glittered and twinkled like a million stars. She was completely transformed.

Needless to say, the other witches immediately banished her from the coven.

And so she became known as Witch Twinkletoes, famous for her herbal teas and healing potions.

Of course, she could never take off the magic boots. Without them she'd lose her good looks. Let's hope there's another pair exactly the same in the little shoe shop in Witch Hollow, for when the soles wear out!

The Witch at the Bottom of the Lane

Katie remembered first meeting the witch at the bottom of the lane when she was just three years old. She had stopped at the gate of a cottage to stroke a black cat and the witch had peered over the hedge at her. She had long, straggly hair and yellow, sharp-looking teeth. Katie had been terrified, imagining the witch was going to eat her. Fortunately, her mum arrived at that moment and the witch disappeared into her cottage and shut the door.

As Katie grew older, she avoided the lane if she could, and never went past the witch's cottage without running. She was never brave enough to stop and stroke the black cat again.

Then one day, Katie and her mother were out shopping in the village.

"Pop into the baker's, will you," said Mum, "and get us some nice chocolate muffins for tea."

There was a queue inside the shop. The baker's cakes were very popular. Katie waited her turn, until at last there was only one old lady in front of her.

"What can I get for you, Mrs Throgmorton?" asked the baker.

"One small brown loaf, please," said the old lady.

"I can't tempt you with one of my chocolate muffins?" joked the baker.

"I'd love to, but I can't afford them," replied Mrs Throgmorton.

Katie was shocked. Fancy not being able to afford a muffin!

"That's terrible!" said Mum, when Katie told her about the old lady. "Why don't we get a couple of muffins for Mrs Throgmorton?"

Katie ran back to the baker's shop, which was still very busy, and by the time she had bought the extra muffins, the old lady was almost out of sight.

Katie and her mother called to her, but she didn't hear them, so they hurried after her in time to see her turn into the lane where the witch lived!

"Oh, no," said Katie. "Must we go down there? I really don't want to go past the witch's house," she pleaded.

"Don't be silly, Katie," said Mum.

Katie was nearly eight now, but she could still remember how frightened she had been all those years ago when the witch had peered at her over the hedge.

She held on tightly to her mother's hand.

"Mrs Throgmorton!" called Katie's mum, and the old lady turned her head.

To Katie's horror, the old lady was opening the gate to the witch's garden!

Mum gave Mrs Throgmorton the muffins and the old lady smiled gratefully. Her face was kind and her smile was warm. How could Katie have thought so badly of her, all this time thinking she was a witch?

"You can imagine the silliest things when you're very young," smiled Mrs Throgmorton, winking at Katie.

From then on, Katie went to visit Mrs Throgmorton every week, always taking a box of delicious cakes for them to share.